Great Expectations

Great Expectations

By Charles Dickens
Adapted by Monica Kulling

Bullseye Step into Classics™

Random House 🏠 New York

A BULLSEYE BOOK PUBLISHED BY RANDOM HOUSE, INC.
Text copyright © 1996 by Random House, Inc.
Cover illustration copyright © 1996 by Bill Dodge
All rights reserved under International and Pan-American Copyright
Conventions. Published in the United States by Random House, Inc.,
New York, and simultaneously in Canada by Random House of Canada
Limited, Toronto.

http://www.randomhouse.com/

Library of Congress Cataloging-in-Publication Data:
Kulling, Monica. Great expectations / by Charles Dickens ; adapted by
Monica Kulling. — 1st Random House Bullseye Books ed.
  p. cm. — (Bullseye step into classics)
SUMMARY: After harsh early years, Pip, an orphan growing up in Victorian
England, is given the means to become a gentleman by an unknown
benefactor and learns that outward appearances can be deceiving.
ISBN 0-679-87466-6 (pbk.)
[1. Orphans—Fiction. 2. England—Fiction.] I. Dickens, Charles,
1812–1870. Great expectations. II. Title. III. Series.
PZ7.K9490155Gr 1996 [Fic]—dc20 95-17616

First Random House Bullseye Books edition: 1996

Printed in the United States of America 10 9 8 7

Contents

Chapter One

Pip

My first memory is of a churchyard. I was only seven years old, and I was frightened of the graves that were all around me. My father and mother were buried there. I began to cry. My sobs filled the churchyard.

"What's that noise?" cried a terrible voice.

A man was hiding behind one of the gravestones!

"Keep still, you little devil, or I'll cut your throat!"

The man came toward me. He was wet and muddy. Leg irons bound his ankles. He limped and shivered and glared and growled. He was an escaped prisoner.

All at once, the stranger grabbed me by the chin.

"Don't cut my throat, sir," I pleaded.

"Tell me your name! Quick!"

"Pip," I said. "Pip, sir."

"Show me where you live," said the man. "Point out the place."

I pointed to our village. It was about a mile from the church and twenty miles from the sea.

Suddenly the man picked me up and turned me upside down! My pockets were empty except for one piece of bread, which fell to the ground.

Then the prisoner sat me on a gravestone. He tore into the bread like a starving animal.

"Boy," he said between bites, "where's your mother?"

"There, sir!" I said, pointing to the gravestone over the man's shoulder.

The man was terrified. He thought my mother was standing behind him!

He started to run past me. Then he

stopped and quickly looked over his shoulder.

"There, sir," I explained, timidly.

I pointed at the gravestone. "That's my mother. And that's my father lying beside her."

"Ha!" he muttered. "Who do you live with, then?"

"My sister, sir—Mrs. Joe Gargery—wife of Joe Gargery, the blacksmith, sir."

"Blacksmith, eh?" he said. He looked down at his leg irons. Then he limped over to me, grabbed my arms, and tilted me backward. He looked powerfully down into my eyes. I looked helplessly up into his.

"Know what a file is?" he demanded.

"Yes, sir."

"You know what wittles is?"

"It's food, sir," I said.

"You get me a file," he said, tilting me farther backward. "And you get me wittles. And I'll let you live."

I was so weak and scared that I clung

to the prisoner with both hands.

He let me go and glared at me.

"You bring me the file and wittles tonight," he said. "And don't say a word to anyone. If you do, I'll tear your heart and liver out and roast them!"

The convict frightened me. At that moment, I would have done anything he asked. I promised to bring the items and to keep quiet. Then I fled the churchyard.

It was dusk. Over the marsh, the wind and the man's words howled together in my ears.

I knew I had to help the convict. If I didn't, he might track me down at Joe's. The only problem was sneaking the food past my sister. She was more than twenty years older than me, and she often lost her temper. If she caught me hiding food, I'd surely be punished.

My sister's husband, Joe, was my friend. He stood up for me when he could. But tonight he gave me away when I tried to hide a piece of bread down my pants leg during supper.

"I say, Pip, old chap," said Joe. "Stop eating so fast. You couldn't have chewed that bread all the way through. You'll make yourself sick."

"What's he done now?" asked my sister, looking up from her plate.

"He's going to choke on his food," said Joe.

"Pip, if you can cough it up, you should," he said. "It's not good manners, but your health's your health.

"I shoveled my food down when I was a boy. But not as fast as you. It's a wonder it hasn't killed you!"

My sister pulled me up by the hair.

"You come and be dosed," she ordered.

My sister's favorite punishment was a dose of tar-water. She gave me a large spoonful. It was a thick, dark, foul-smelling liquid. It tasted like mud. I forced it down without a word.

Later that night, while everyone

slept, I tiptoed into the kitchen and snuck into the pantry. I grabbed the first thing I saw. It was a pork pie Joe's Uncle Pumblechook had brought for tomorrow's Christmas dinner. Then I took some brandy and a file from Joe's workshop. I ran to the churchyard. I couldn't wait to deliver the supplies and be done with the convict.

The convict was happy to see me. I gave him the items he wanted and raced back home. I fell into a fitful sleep, huddled under my blanket. The shrill sound of a file scraping leg irons cut through my dreams.

The next day was Christmas. Mr. Wopsle, the clerk at the church, was dining with us. Joe's Uncle Pumblechook was also there.

I sat at the table and worried. Soon my sister would find out that the brandy and the pork pie were gone. Then I would really be in trouble!

Dinner went on and on. I began to think I might survive the night. Then my sister said, "I almost forgot! Uncle Pumblechook gave us a pork pie."

She went to the pantry to get the pie, but she returned with an empty plate.

"Gracious me," she said. "It's gone. The pie is gone."

I couldn't stand the guilt another minute. I had to get out of there. I jumped up from the table and threw open the front door. A group of soldiers was standing on our porch. One, the sergeant, held out a pair of handcuffs.

"We need a blacksmith to fix these for us," he said. "Two convicts have escaped the Hulks. We're going to find them."

The Hulks were the prison ships moored near the marsh. So there were *two* convicts—not just the one I had helped!

Joe fired up the forge and fixed the

handcuffs. He wanted to join the hunt. So did Mr. Wopsle and Uncle Pumblechook.

We started off across the marshes, climbing up banks and down ditches. I sat high atop Joe's shoulders. I looked through the thick fog, hoping to spot my convict first.

I knew he would think I had given him away. He would find me and roast me for sure!

Suddenly we heard shouting. The sergeant ran on ahead. Joe put me down, and we followed him.

My convict was fighting a man who had a long scar across his face. I stood at the edge of the ditch. I wanted my convict to see me.

The soldiers broke up the fight and handcuffed the two men. As they were led away, my convict looked at me. I shook my head slightly. I was trying to tell him that I had kept my promise.

There was no anger, only interest, in

his eyes. I did not understand the look. Then he turned to the sergeant.

"I stole a pork pie and some brandy from the blacksmith's," he said.

"We *were* missing a pie," said Joe. "Remember, Pip?" Then he said to my convict, "Whatever you've done, we wouldn't want you to starve. Would we, Pip?"

I did not reply. By the light of the torches, I saw the black Hulks lying near the muddy shore.

The prisoners were rowed to the ship and taken up. The torches were tossed, hissing, into the water.

I went home with the memory of that night burned into my brain forever.

Chapter Two

Estella

Mr. Wopsle's great-aunt ran an elementary school in the village. The classes were held at night. Mr. Wopsle's great-aunt was old and always fell asleep in front of the class. Her students paid two pennies a week to watch her sleep. But sometimes Biddy, her granddaughter, took over.

Biddy was an orphan. Her hair often needed brushing and her hands needed washing, but she had a good heart. If it weren't for Biddy, I never would have learned to read or write.

One winter evening, a year after the hunt for the convict, I sat by the fire writing on a slate. My sister was out with Mr. Pumblechook.

I wrote to Joe even though he was sitting beside me:

"mI deEr JO i opE U R kWite wEll. i opE i shAl soN B aBelL 2 teeDge U 2 ritE JO."

"I say, Pip, old chap!" cried Joe, opening his blue eyes wide. "What a scholar you are! Ain't you?"

"I would like to be," I said, smiling at the letters on the slate.

When I got older, Joe was going to teach me his trade. I loved Joe dearly, but the thought of working in the forge made my heart heavy. I wanted a different kind of life. I dreamed about being rich, having nice clothes, and spending every day reading books and learning.

Suddenly my sister interrupted my daydreams. She burst into the room with Mr. Pumblechook.

"Now," she said, undoing her coat

quickly, "if this boy ain't grateful this night, he never will be! I only hope she doesn't pamper him."

"She's not like that," said Mr. Pumblechook. "She's definitely not the type to pamper."

"Who's not the type?" asked Joe. "Who is *she?*" Joe looked at me.

"Miss Havisham," replied my sister impatiently. "She wants Pip to play with a girl who's living with her. She might even pay him. He better go, or he'll answer to me."

"I wonder how Miss Havisham knows our Pip," said Joe, astounded.

"Noodlehead!" cried my sister. "Who said she knew him?"

"Well, how else could she know about Pip?" asked Joe, politely.

"Our dear Uncle Pumblechook is a neighbor of hers," began my sister. "Perhaps she asked him if he knew a boy just like Pip. And then our thoughtful, kind Uncle Pumblechook mentioned this boy!"

My sister waved a hand in my direction. Mr. Pumblechook puffed out his chest and stared up at the ceiling. He was proud that he knew Miss Havisham.

"This boy could earn a fortune by going to Miss Havisham's. He should be grateful," said my sister.

I wasn't grateful at all. I was nervous. Miss Havisham was a rich and grim lady who lived at the edge of town in a large and cheerless house. People said she never went outside. I didn't want to meet the strange woman—or spend every day with her. The whole idea sounded terrible.

But I didn't have much choice in the matter. The next day my sister shooed me out the door at dawn. I slowly walked across town to the iron gates of Miss Havisham's house with Mr. Pumblechook by my side. A servant answered the bell and opened the gate. She slammed it after me.

"She don't want to see *you*," the woman announced to Mr. Pumblechook.

I followed her through the courtyard and the dark hallways of the house. We climbed a staircase and came, at last, to a door.

The servant knocked and said, "Go in." Then she pushed me into the room and closed the door behind me.

The room was large and well lit by candles. In an armchair sat Miss Havisham—the strangest lady I had ever seen.

Miss Havisham was dressed all in white. A long veil covered her head. Jewels glittered on her neck and hands. She was dressed for a wedding.

Even her hair was white. Her face was pale and withered. It seemed as if she had dressed for a wedding many years ago and had grown old since. She looked like a wax figure in a museum!

"Who is it?" asked the lady.

"Pip, ma'am," I replied.

"Pip?"

"Mr. Pumblechook's boy, ma'am. I've come to play," I explained.

"Come closer," said Miss Havisham. "Are you afraid of a woman who has not seen the sun since before you were born?"

I was terrified, but said nothing. I stepped closer. I saw that Miss Havisham's watch had stopped at twenty minutes to nine. The clock in the room also read twenty minutes to nine.

"Do you know what I touch here?" she said, laying her hand on the left side of her chest.

"Your heart," I said.

"Broken!" she cried.

A strange smile lit her face.

"I am tired," said Miss Havisham. "I want to watch you play. A girl lives with me here. Her name is Estella. Call for her."

I opened the door and shouted down

the dark hall for Estella. I called again, and waited. At last, I saw a light like a star moving along the dark passage.

A young girl entered the room. She walked over to Miss Havisham, who placed a jewel against the girl's pretty brown hair.

"It shall be yours one day," Miss Havisham told Estella. "You shall wear it well. Now, let me see you play cards with this boy."

"With *this* boy?" asked the girl. Her pretty face soured with scorn.

"This is a common laboring boy!" she added.

Miss Havisham whispered softly to her, "You can break his heart."

We sat down to cards. Estella dealt. When she was finished, I picked up my cards.

"What rough hands he has!" she said. "And what thick boots! What a clumsy-looking boy he is!"

The girl was my own age, but she acted much older. She looked down on me as though she were a queen and I was dirt on her shoe.

I had never been ashamed of myself before. But now I realized she was right. My clothes were dirty. My hair was tangled. As I played the game, I hid my hands behind the cards.

Estella won the first game. I dealt the second. I was so nervous that I made a mistake, and she called me stupid.

I didn't know what to say, so I said nothing.

"You said nothing back," remarked Miss Havisham, as she looked on. "She says many harsh things, but you say nothing. What do you think of her? Tell me in my ear."

"I think she is very proud," I replied in a whisper.

"Anything else?"

"I think she is very pretty."

I looked over at Estella. She was frowning.

"Anything else?" asked Miss Havisham.

"I think she is very insulting," I said. "And I should like to go home."

It was enough for one day.

Estella left me in the courtyard. As she closed the front door, I saw a look of hatred pass across her face.

I felt so hurt and bitter. I leaned my head against a stone wall and cried. I kicked the wall and twisted my hair. But I was not alone in the courtyard.

"Who let *you* in?" asked a tall, thin boy.

"Miss Estella."

"Come and fight," said the young gentleman.

He took off his jacket and put his fists up. He danced around me like a boxer in a ring. Secretly, I was afraid of him.

My first day at Miss Havisham's

ended in a fistfight. I hit the young man twice in the face and he fell.

"That means you have won," he said, calmly.

He seemed so brave and innocent. I didn't feel as if I had won. My heart was heavy. I knew cruel Estella would make my visits unbearable.

Chapter Three

Great Expectations

For the next few months, I visited Miss Havisham every day. Each time, mean Estella teased and taunted me. But I was fascinated by her. I could not bear to be away from her.

On one visit Miss Havisham was waiting for me in a wheelchair. She wanted me to push her around her bedroom, then across the landing and into the room next door.

This room was filled with dust and cobwebs. A long table was set for a wedding feast. Mice nibbled on a rotten wedding cake lying in the center of the table. By now I was used to Miss Havisham's strange ways. This bizarre room didn't even surprise me.

Miss Havisham was quiet at first. She talked more as she got used to me. She asked me what I was learning and what I wanted to be when I grew up. I told her I would soon become Joe's apprentice.

I told her the blacksmith's trade did not interest me. I wanted to be a gentleman and live in a big city.

Secretly, I hoped Miss Havisham would help me. But she never paid me money. I spent time with Estella. In return, Miss Havisham gave me dinner. That was all.

One day Miss Havisham asked me to bring Joe to her.

"You are growing tall, Pip!" she said. "You should be learning your life's trade from a master."

I brought Joe to Miss Havisham's room the very next day. Joe was nervous. He twisted his cap in his hands. He looked at me when he answered Miss Havisham's questions.

"You raised this boy to be your apprentice," began Miss Havisham. "Is that right, Mr. Gargery?"

"You know, Pip," replied Joe, looking at me, "we've always been friends. It would be a lark to work together. You want to, don't you, Pip?"

I tried to get Joe to speak to Miss Havisham instead of me, but he wouldn't. His shyness made me ashamed. Especially when I saw that Estella was laughing at us.

"I want you to be Mr. Gargery's apprentice. Here is some money," said Miss Havisham. She dropped a sack of coins into my hand.

"You have earned it, Pip. Give the money to your new master. You will make a fine blacksmith one day."

After that day my visits ended. I took my place at the forge. I welded horseshoes, buckets, and machinery. My heavy heart made the hammers and tools I worked on seem as light as a feather.

I lived in fear that one day Estella would peek in the window and see me working. My hands and face would be black from coal. Estella would despise me more than she already did. Then she would run away in disgust—and I would never see her again.

One day blended into another. About a year later, I asked Joe if I could visit Miss Havisham.

"She might think you want something," he replied.

"But I have never thanked her or shown that I remember her," I said.

I missed my visits to that strange house. Most of all, I missed Estella.

"Since we aren't so busy right now, Joe," I said, "I would like to take half a day off tomorrow and call on Miss Est—Havisham."

"Her name ain't Estavisham," said Joe, with a twinkle in his eye. "Unless someone has given her a new name."

"I know, Joe, I know," I said. "But may I go?"

Joe gave me the time off. Orlick, Joe's other worker, demanded the same. But my sister told Joe not to give it to him. My sister did not like Orlick. She thought he was lazy. She and Orlick were always fighting. In the end, Joe gave Orlick the time off to keep him happy.

I couldn't wait to see Estella again. I scrubbed the grit from my hands and put on my clothes with the least patches and tears.

When I arrived at Miss Havisham's, she told me that Estella was in Europe.

"She's getting an education," said Miss Havisham. "She's prettier than ever, and admired by all who see her. Do you feel that you have lost her?"

I didn't know what to say. I left Miss Havisham's more unhappy about my home and my life than ever before.

A heavy mist hung in the air. Around a bend in the road, I met Orlick.

"The guns are going again," he said.

"At the Hulks?" I asked.

"Aye!" he replied. "Some of the birds have flown their cages!"

I immediately remembered the night in the graveyard with my convict.

I was almost home when a neighbor ran up to me.

"Convicts broke into your house when Gargery was out. Somebody was attacked and hurt!" he cried.

I ran straight home. Practically the whole village was in our yard. I found Joe and a doctor in the kitchen. My sister was lying on the floor. She looked as if she was dead. She had been hit many times on her head and back. Leg irons lay beside her. They had been filed through—a long time ago, Joe said.

They were my convict's irons. But somehow I knew my convict didn't do this terrible thing. The attacker must have found the irons in the churchyard!

Orlick hated my sister. He was the only man capable of such a dreadful crime, but there was no evidence to prove him guilty.

I felt responsible because I had provided the weapon. For months, I wanted to tell Joe the story. But every day I kept silent.

My sister lived, but never spoke again. Instead, she wrote messages on a slate. Now it took her a long time to understand things, and she became a patient and gentle woman. She never lost her temper again. She was sometimes unhappy, but never angry.

Biddy, the schoolteacher's granddaughter, came to live with us. She helped me and Joe watch over my sister and tend to the household chores. Biddy was clever and kind, but not as outwardly beautiful as Estella. Her beauty was inside.

How I wished I could love her as I loved Estella. I knew my life would be less painful if I could fall in love with simple, good-hearted Biddy.

Chapter Four

Leaving Home

Four years later, a lawyer from London paid me a visit. I was still working with Joe in the forge. The lawyer's name was Mr. Jaggers. His news would change my life.

"Joseph Gargery, my client would like to take this young fellow off your hands," he said. "He will be taken care of for the rest of his life. I am prepared to pay you for your loss."

"I won't take money," said Joe. "I would never stand in Pip's way. If there is another future for Pip, he is free to go."

Mr. Jaggers then turned to me.

"You will soon receive a handsome

sum," he said. "The person giving you this money wants you to be brought up as a gentleman—as a young fellow of great expectations."

My dream had come true! I was so excited that I hardly heard what the lawyer said next.

"Two conditions come with the gift," said Mr. Jaggers. "You must keep the name Pip, and your benefactor's name must be a secret. It will be told to you in time.

"Everything has been arranged," continued Mr. Jaggers. "You will move to London. There you will be taught by Mr. Matthew Pocket and live with his son, Herbert."

I knew that the Pockets were relatives of Miss Havisham. She must be my benefactor!

Mr. Jaggers tossed a bag of coins on the workbench.

"Buy new clothes," he ordered, looking me up and down. "You shouldn't come to London dressed in work clothes."

"I am thunderstruck," said Joe.

So was I. In my heart, I knew it was terrible to be so happy. I *wanted* to leave my dear, good Joe.

"The sooner you leave, the better," said Mr. Jaggers. "Take a coach to London in one week and meet me at my office."

He handed me his card and left.

Joe and I ran to the house to tell Biddy the good news.

My sister was sitting in her chair in the corner. Biddy was sitting closer to the fire, sewing.

Joe burst into the room. He slapped his hat on the table.

"Pip is now a gentleman of fortune," he announced, "and God bless him in it!"

Biddy dropped her work and looked at me. Joe smiled at me. After a moment they both congratulated me. But there was a sadness in their words that made me angry. Why couldn't they be more happy for me? After all, this was the chance I had been waiting for all my life.

At supper Joe and Biddy kept congratulating me. "You're going to be a gentleman," they said over and over. They seemed unable to believe that such a good thing could happen to me. Somehow I didn't like that much.

That night, I lay on my bed feeling sad and lost. I couldn't understand it. On the first night of my bright fortunes, I felt lonelier than ever.

I wondered if Miss Havisham had plans for me to marry Estella. This thought cheered me up, and I fell into a deep sleep.

The next day I ordered new clothes from the tailor. They were made from the finest materials I had ever seen. They were also very expensive. The clothes cost more money than Joe earned in one month! Joe and Biddy were impressed when I showed them off.

"I want to say good-bye to Miss Havisham," I told them, and hurried across town.

When I arrived, Miss Havisham was using a cane to walk around the wedding feast room. She saw me and stopped at the rotten cake.

"I have come into such good fortune since I last saw you, Miss Havisham," I said. "I am so grateful!"

I made sure not to let on that I thought she was my benefactor.

"Aye!" replied Miss Havisham. "Mr. Jaggers told me the news, Pip. So you are adopted by a rich person?"

"Yes, Miss Havisham."

"Not named?"

"No, Miss Havisham."

"And Mr. Jaggers is your guardian?"

"Yes, Miss Havisham."

"Well, you have a promising career before you," she said. "Good-bye, Pip! You will always keep the name of Pip, you know."

She stretched out her hand. I went down on one knee and put her hand to my lips. There seemed to be no other way to thank her.

On the morning of my trip to London, I hurried through breakfast. I was scared and excited at the same time. I couldn't wait to become a gentleman.

I kissed my sister good-bye. Biddy had tried to tell her about my good fortune. My sister laughed and nodded as if she understood.

I kissed Biddy and threw my arms around Joe. Then I quickly left.

I walked by myself to the village. If I boarded the coach there, no one would see Joe's run-down house.

On the way, I broke down in tears.

"Good-bye, my dear friend Joe!" I

whispered as the coach rolled into the countryside. My heart ached at leaving him.

But each mile took me farther away from regret. The adventure of my life lay ahead of me!

Chapter Five

Miss Havisham's Story

The trip to London took five hours, but it only seemed like five minutes. It was a little past noon when the four-horse coach rolled into the crowded streets of the big city.

I was dropped off at Jaggers's office in a gloomy part of the city. I entered the front office and asked for Mr. Jaggers.

"He is in court at present," said the clerk. "Are you Mr. Pip?"

I said I was and he immediately grabbed his coat and hat.

"We have been expecting your arrival. Mr. Jaggers told me to take you to your new home," the clerk said, leading me through the narrow, cobbled streets.

We arrived at a neat little house. MR. POCKET, JUNIOR was painted on the front door and on the mailbox.

"This is it," said the clerk. "I think you'll find everything in order." The clerk left, and I climbed the stairs.

The front door was unlocked. I entered and looked around the rooms. I was writing my name in the dirt on a windowpane when I heard footsteps on the stairs.

A young man entered, carrying two bags of groceries.

"Mr. Pip?" he asked.

"Mr. Pocket?" I replied.

I looked into the man's familiar face. He looked into mine.

"Well, I'll be," he said. "You're the boy I fought in Miss Havisham's court-yard!"

"And so are you," I said, and laughed.

"I heard you'd come into good for-tune," said Herbert. "When I first met you, I'd been invited to play with Estella. It turned out that Miss Havisham didn't like me. But I don't care. She's a terror!"

"Miss Havisham?" I asked.

"I meant Estella. Miss Havisham taught her to hate men," he said.

Over dinner, Herbert told me Miss Havisham's story.

"Her father was a rich man. He had a daughter, Miss Havisham, by his first wife and a son by his second.

"His son turned out badly. When Mr. Havisham died, he left his son just a little money. He gave most of the inheritance to Miss Havisham.

"Her brother hated her for it," Herbert continued. "He convinced a friend to pretend to love her. The friend asked Miss Havisham to marry him. She accepted.

"The day was set, the dress bought, and the guests invited. But the bridegroom never showed up. He wrote a letter to Miss Havisham that said he wouldn't marry her."

Now I knew why Miss Havisham's clocks were stopped.

"She must have received the letter when she was dressing for her wedding...at twenty minutes to nine!" I exclaimed.

"At that very hour and minute," said Herbert. "She stopped all the clocks, and never left the house again!"

"You say Estella is not related to Miss Havisham," I said. "When was she adopted by her?"

Herbert shrugged his shoulders.

"I don't know," he said. "You know as much as I do now."

The next day my studies began. Mr. Matthew Pocket, Herbert's father, was an excellent teacher. He taught me everything about being a gentleman. He gave me wonderful books to read— adventure stories, plays, essays, mysteries, and even comedies. He also showed me which clothes and shoes to buy, and he helped me decorate my room. He taught me how to act at parties. And Herbert taught me table manners!

There were two other students in Mr. Pocket's small class, Bentley Drummle and Startop. Drummle was a nasty fellow. He was lazy and proud. I didn't like him at all.

Startop was open and warm. We became friends. We went rowing in the evenings. Startop and I rowed my boat while Drummle rowed his own far behind us.

One evening, Mr. Jaggers decided he wanted to meet my fellow students. He invited the three of us to his home for dinner.

Startop, Drummle, and I met in front of Jaggers's house. It was impressive in size, but it needed painting and window cleaning.

We knocked on the door, and Jaggers

led us into the dining room. The table was already set for dinner.

"Pip," said Mr. Jaggers, putting his hand on my shoulder. "Who are these fine young men?"

I introduced Drummle and Startop and we all sat down to eat.

Jaggers seemed to take to Drummle immediately. They spoke quietly between themselves.

The housekeeper entered with the first course. She was about forty, tall and nimble. Her face was pale. Her large eyes were sad. But I sensed a fire beneath her quietness.

Each time she returned with a new dish, I watched her. There was something familiar about her, but I couldn't put my finger on it. I was sure I had never seen her before.

The evening came to an early end.

"I am glad to see you all," said Mr. Jaggers. "Mr. Drummle, I drink to you. You will go far in life."

I was astounded that a man as shrewd as Mr. Jaggers could be taken in by the sly Drummle. It turned out that he would not be the only one.

Chapter Six

A Visit from Joe

One Monday morning I got a letter from Biddy.

> *My dear Mr. Pip:*
> *Mr. Gargery asked me to write. He is going to London and would like to see you. He will call for you on Tuesday morning at nine o'clock.*
> *—Biddy*

> *P.S. I hope you will see him, even though you are now a gentleman. You have such a good heart, and he is a worthy, worthy man.*

Joe would be here tomorrow! I did not want to see him. He did not fit in with my new life. If I could have kept him away, I would have. Biddy was wrong. My heart was anything but good.

I got up early Tuesday morning to clean my newly decorated rooms.

Soon I heard Joe on the stairs. I knew it was Joe by his clumsy walk. His boots were too big for him.

I greeted Joe at the door. He was wearing his best suit—the one he only wore to weddings and funerals. He wiped his feet over and over on the mat. I thought I would have to lift him off it to stop him.

"Joe, how are you?" I asked.

"Pip, how are you?" he replied.

His face glowed with happiness. He came in and put his hat on the floor. He took both my hands and shook them up and down, as if I were a water pump!

"I am glad to see you, Joe," I said. "Give me your hat."

But Joe didn't want to part with his hat. He picked it up with both hands as if it were a bird's nest filled with eggs. He talked while awkwardly holding the hat.

"You've grown," said Joe. "To be sure, you are an honor to your king and country."

Joe's words made me uncomfortable. He wasn't acting like his old self.

I introduced Joe to Herbert, who held out his hand. Joe backed away from it. He clutched his hat tighter.

"Your servant, sir," said Joe, bowing slightly.

"Do you take tea or coffee, Mr. Gargery?" asked Herbert.

"Thankee, sir," said Joe, stiff from head to foot. "I'll have whatever you're having."

"How about coffee?" suggested Herbert.

"Thankee, sir," returned Joe, clearly unhappy with the choice. "You are kind to offer, but don't you find coffee a little heating?"

"How about tea, then?" asked Herbert, pouring it out.

Joe put his hat on the mantel and sat down to breakfast.

I was glad when Herbert left for work. Having the two of them at the same table made me nervous. I was impatient with Joe's ways and I'm afraid he knew it.

"Now that we're alone, sir—" began Joe.

"Joe," I interrupted, "how can you call me sir? You're like a father to me."

"Now that we're alone," Joe began again, "I can tell you that I have a message from Miss Havisham."

"Miss Havisham?" I asked with surprise.

"Estella is home and would be glad to see you."

I felt my face grow hot. If I had known Joe had this message for me, I would have been kinder to him, I'm sure.

Joe stood and picked up his hat.

"I wish you well and hope you prosper to greater and greater heights," he said.

"But where are you going? Aren't you coming back for dinner, Joe?" I asked.

"No, I am not," he said. "Pip, dear old chap, life has parted us. I'm wrong in these clothes. I'm wrong out of the forge and away from the marshes. You and me should not be together in London. God bless you, dear old Pip, God bless you!"

Joe put his hat on. Then he touched me gently on the forehead and left.

Chapter Seven

Good-Bye to Mrs. Joe

The next day I caught a coach for the marsh. I knew I *should* stay at Joe's. It would make up for our horrible visit in the city. But I remembered how awkward things were between us and decided to stay at the Blue Boar Inn instead.

In the morning, I did not go to Joe's. I walked over to Miss Havisham's side of town and thought about Estella.

Miss Havisham had adopted her. She had practically adopted me. She must want to bring us together! My heart was light with hope when I rang the bell on the iron gate.

Miss Havisham had a new porter. It was Orlick. Joe had fired him.

"Ah, young master," Orlick said with a sneer. "There's more changes than yours in the world."

Without saying a word, I walked past him. I crossed the gloomy courtyard and entered the house. Miss Havisham was sitting in the banquet room. Her hands were crossed on top of her cane.

"I heard that you wanted to see me," I said. "I came as quickly as I could."

A lady I did not know stood before the fire. She turned around. It was Estella!

She had changed! She was even more beautiful than before. I felt as if I had not changed at all. I was still the same coarse and common boy.

"Has he changed?" Miss Havisham asked Estella.

"Very much," she replied, looking at me.

Suddenly she kissed Miss Havisham's hand and left the room.

"Isn't she beautiful and graceful?"

Miss Havisham asked with a greedy look. She put an arm around my neck and pulled me close to her.

"Love her, love her, love her!" Miss Havisham whispered in my ear. "If she favors you, love her. If she hurts you, love her. If she tears your heart to pieces, love her!"

I had never heard anyone talk like this before. It scared me.

"Hear me, Pip!" she continued. "I adopted her to be loved. I brought her up to be loved. I made her what she is today. Love her! Love her!"

Miss Havisham ranted like a madwoman. Her cries cut the musty air of the room. She made the word "love" sound like a curse.

"Go, Pip!" she said, pointing her cane at the door. "Go into the garden. Walk with her!"

Estella and I did as she said. In the garden, Estella walked and talked like a lady. I felt like a little boy beside her—

not the gentleman I thought I had become. I could see that I wasn't important to her. She probably never thought about me while she was away.

"I have no heart," said Estella suddenly. "Oh, my heart can be stabbed or shot. My heart can stop beating, but it cannot be touched. There is no softness, no tenderness in me."

Her cold voice was like Miss Havisham's. But her face and hands reminded me of someone else. It was someone I had just met, but I could not remember where.

I left for London without seeing Joe. My mind was crowded with thoughts of Estella. Miss Havisham's words kept ringing in my ears. I was miserable by the time I got home.

A few months later my sister died, and I went to the funeral. When I arrived, the house was full of mourners. Poor dear Joe was sitting by himself in a corner of the living room. He was wrapped in a black cloak tied at the chin with a large bow. He looked as uncomfortable as he had in London.

I bent down to him. "Dear Joe, how are you?"

"Pip, old boy," he said. "You knew her when she was a fine fig…a fine figure…of…of a woman."

Then he broke down in tears.

My sister was buried in the churchyard beside our mother and father. The larks sang and a light wind blew away the clouds over our heads.

I said farewell to the woman who had brought me up.

My twenty-first birthday came, and with it a larger yearly income from my benefactor.

On that day, I asked Mr. Jaggers who that benefactor was.

"You will know when your benefactor chooses to tell you," replied Mr. Jaggers.

I couldn't understand why Miss Havisham wanted to keep the secret. Then I heard some shocking news. Drummle was courting Estella! I left for Miss Havisham's the next day.

Chapter Eight

Estella's Cold Heart

Miss Havisham was seated near the fire, with Estella at her feet, when I arrived. Light from the fire shone on their faces.

Estella was upset. Suddenly she flung her knitting aside and stood up.

"What!" cried Miss Havisham, her eyes flashing. "Are you tired of me?"

"Only a little tired of myself," replied Estella, with a sigh. She stood at the hearth and looked into the fire.

"Speak the truth, you ingrate!" cried Miss Havisham, striking her cane on the floor. "You are tired of me. I know it!"

Estella did not answer. Miss Havisham's face was red with rage.

"You are like stone!" she shouted. "You cold, cold heart!"

"What!" replied Estella. "You think *I'm* cold?"

"Are you not?" asked Miss Havisham.

I was shocked by the argument. Miss Havisham never spoke to Estella like this. And Estella was never so cruel to Miss Havisham.

"I am what you have made me," said Estella. "Take all the praise. Take all the blame."

"Oh, look at her, Pip," said Miss Havisham bitterly. "Look at her, so hard and thankless. Did I never give her love?"

Miss Havisham's words did not affect Estella at all.

"So proud, so proud!" cried Miss Havisham. She grabbed her white hair and pulled it.

"Who taught me to be so proud and so hard?" demanded Estella. "Who praised me when I learned the lessons well? It is your fault I am this way."

"But to be proud and hard to *me!*" cried Miss Havisham, stretching her arms out to Estella.

Estella looked at Miss Havisham calmly. Then she fixed her gaze on the fire once more.

"How can you expect me to be anything more than what I am? You were the one who taught me that love is an enemy."

Miss Havisham's hands fell limply into her lap. Her head hung. She moaned and swayed in her chair. Then, suddenly, she was quiet. Estella returned to her knitting. The storm had come and gone so quickly, I hardly knew what had happened.

Miss Havisham stared silently into the fire. I chose that moment to confront Estella.

"Estella, tell me why are you seeing Drummle," I said. "You know he is an ill-tempered, stupid fellow and not worthy of you. How can you be with him?"

"Moths and other ugly creatures come to the light of a candle," replied Estella. "Can the candle help it?"

"No," I said, "but *you* could if you wanted to."

Estella's face turned to the fire. Now was my chance!

"Estella," I said nervously, "I have loved you ever since I first saw you in this house."

Miss Havisham put her hand to her heart as she looked at us.

"I know you will never be mine, Estella," I continued. "Still, I love you."

"Those are only words," said Estella. "You touch nothing in my heart. I warned you of this, did I not?"

I nodded. I felt miserable.

"It is true that Bentley Drummle visits me," said Estella. "In fact, he is dining here tonight."

"Do you love him, Estella? Will you marry him?" I asked.

I feared the worst. Drummle was mean. Estella's life with him would be horrible. Marrying him would be a mistake.

"What have I told you?" she replied. "Love means nothing to me. But, yes, I am going to marry him."

I covered my face with my hands. All was lost.

"Estella, do not do this!" I cried. "What Miss Havisham has taught you is wrong. She only wants revenge. You must not ruin your life for her sake!"

"I'm going to be married soon," said Estella. "It has nothing to do with my adoptive mother! It is my own act. I want to change my life. Say no more. We will never understand each other."

"Drummle is a mean, stupid brute!" I shouted. I was desperate.

"Don't think I will make Bentley's

life a happy one," said Estella. "Come! Here is my hand. Let us part friends."

"Oh, Estella," I said.

But there was no use in pleading. I held her hand to my lips. My bitter tears fell onto her smooth skin. I knew in my soul that whatever happened, Estella would always be a part of me.

Chapter Nine

My Benefactor

By my twenty-third birthday, I still did not know the name of my benefactor. Herbert and I were living at Garden Court, down by the river.

Outside, a storm had been raging for days. The wind and rain drenched everything in its path. Today had been the worst of all.

I stayed indoors all day. I tried to keep busy. In the evening, I sat in my room reading. Herbert was in France on business. I missed his cheerful face.

Suddenly I heard a footstep on the stair.

I took my reading lamp into the hall. The footsteps stopped.

"Is someone down there?" I called.

"Yes," said a voice from the darkness below.

"What floor do you want?" I asked.

"I want Mr. Pip's floor," the stranger replied.

"I am Mr. Pip," I said.

I held the lamp over the railing, and the man came up the stairs. I could not see his face, but I could see that he wore seaman's clothes. His hair was long and gray. He looked about sixty years old.

The man climbed the last stair. He looked at me as if he knew me. I did not recognize him.

"What is your business?" I asked.

"My business?" repeated the man. "I will tell you."

The seaman entered my room and looked around with pleasure. He took off his coat and hat and held out both his hands to me.

"What do you want?" I asked. I feared he might be crazy.

"I have waited many years for this

day, and come so far. Give me a minute, please."

He sat down and covered his forehead with one hand. Suddenly he looked over his shoulder.

"There's no one here with you, is there?" he asked nervously.

"How can you, a stranger, come into my room and ask that question?"

"You're a game one," he replied, shaking his head fondly at me. "I'm glad you growed up a game one!"

Suddenly his face became familiar to me. It was the man in the graveyard! I stood face to face with my convict!

He stood and held out his hands once again. I did not know what to do. I put my hands in his. He grabbed them.

"You acted nobly, my boy," he said. "Noble Pip! I have never forgotten what you did for me in the churchyard!"

I pulled away. I was afraid he might hug me.

"Keep away!" I said. "I don't need

thanks for what I did for you when I was a child. Just live a changed life. That is all the thanks I need."

I could see that my words hurt him. I tried to soften them.

"You are wet and tired. Will you have a drink before you go?" I offered.

I made my convict some hot rum-and-water. I did not want him to stay long, so I stood while he drank.

My convict told me what had happened to him after we parted. He escaped the Hulks a second time and made his way to Australia, where he became a sheep farmer. He made a lot of money.

"And you've done well, too," he said. "How?"

I started to tremble. "I—have a benefactor," I said.

"By chance, does your yearly income start with the number five?" he asked.

My heart beat like a heavy hammer. My yearly income was five hundred pounds! But how could the convict know that? We hadn't seen each other since that fateful night in the marsh.

"You had a guardian before you turned twenty-one," he continued. "Could the first letter of that man's last name be a J? Could the man's name be Jaggers?"

I could not speak. I could hardly breathe. The horrible truth became clear to me. This convict was my benefactor!

"Yes, Pip, dear boy, I've made a gentleman of you!" the convict said. "I swore I would. I lived rough so you could live smooth. I worked hard so you wouldn't have to work. Pip, you are the gentleman I could never be!"

I recoiled from him as if he were a snake. It pained me to know that a criminal had paid for the life I lived.

My great expectations were dust. Miss Havisham wasn't my benefactor. Estella was never intended for me. It was all a dream! What hurt the most was knowing that I had deserted Joe—for a convict.

The convict took my hands again. My blood ran cold.

"Where will I stay?" he asked. "I must stay somewhere, dear boy."

"To sleep?"

"Yes. To sleep long and sound, for I've been at sea months and months."

I gave the man Herbert's room. Even though I despised him, I could not let him wander the streets.

My sleep that night was filled with nightmares.

At breakfast the convict told me his name was Abel Magwitch. Then he dropped a thick wallet onto the table. It was full of money!

"It's all yours, dear boy," he said. "Buy horses. I won't have my gentleman walking in the mud. Buy horses to ride and horses to drive!"

"Stop!" I cried. "I don't want your

money. I want to know if the police are looking for you and how long you will be staying. You're only visiting, aren't you?"

"I've come for good," he said, lighting his pipe. "I can disguise myself, but the police will hang me if I'm caught. You tell me where I'll live."

I hid Magwitch in my room. When Herbert got home, I told him the whole story. The convict shoved a Bible at him.

"Take it in your right hand," he said. "Swear you won't tell a soul you saw me. Kiss it!"

Now Herbert shared my awful secret. Our life together had taken a terrible turn.

Chapter Ten

The Other Convict

"You must get him out of England," Herbert told me when we were alone. "You will have to go with him, or else he won't go."

As long as Magwitch lived in England, I was not free. I knew how much he wanted me to be "his gentleman." I could not play the part anymore. I decided never to take another penny from this man. But I couldn't let Magwitch be captured. He had done so much for me. I could not let him die.

Magwitch stayed in the privacy of our rooms all day. He only slipped outside for some fresh air at night, under cover of darkness.

One night, the gatekeeper told me he had seen a man with a scar watching our place. He had a rough-looking face and tattered clothes. He skulked around our house and under our windows.

He must be after Magwitch! I thought.

The very next morning, I asked Magwitch about the scar-faced man.

Magwitch filled his pipe and started his story.

"The man's name is Compeyson. I met him at the races years ago. He was a gentleman. He knew how to dress. But he was no better than a common thief!

"Compeyson took me on as a partner. He set up the swindles—and the forgery, and the stolen money—and I did the dirty work. He had brains, but no heart!

"When we were caught, Compeyson looked like a gentleman. I looked like a common wretch. He swore the only guilty one was me. He got seven years, while I got fourteen. I swore I would smash his face one day!"

Magwitch pounded his fist on the table. He stopped to catch his breath.

"I escaped the prison ship, and so did Compeyson. I caught him on the marshes, and we fought the night I first met you. I made sure he was sent back to the Hulks. I never heard from him again."

Magwitch told me that Compeyson was a friend of Miss Havisham's half-brother. *He* was the man who'd pretended to love her. He was the one who left her on her wedding day!

The pieces of this strange puzzle were starting to fit together.

Herbert and I had to get Magwitch away from Compeyson. In a week, we moved him to Herbert's girlfriend's house at Mill Pond Bank. He would be safer there. The house was right on the river. Magwitch and I were catching a steamer out of England. Our escape would be fast and easy.

Every evening I rowed past the house. I watched for a signal from Herbert. Herbert would tell us when it was safe to go.

One day Mr. Jaggers invited me to dinner, and I accepted.

I took a coach to Jaggers's house. Molly, the housekeeper, served the food as soon as I got there.

"Miss Havisham sent me a note, Mr. Pip," said my host. "She wishes to see you. You'll go, won't you?"

I planned to go the next day. Jaggers had more news. Drummle and Estella were married! I had been so busy with Magwitch that I had forgotten all about them!

Molly brought out the dessert. Again she reminded me of someone I knew. Her eyes and the way she moved her hands reminded me of—Estella! Could this be Estella's real mother?

I couldn't stop thinking about Molly and Estella all night. I left Jaggers's house early and went home.

When the sun finally rose, I took the coach to Miss Havisham's house. It was gray and bleak. The garden was in ruins. The paths were overgrown. Most sad of all was the thought that Estella was gone. She was Mrs. Drummle now. She would never live with Miss Havisham again.

Miss Havisham sat in the banquet room. She looked so lonely that I almost felt sorry for her.

"Who is it?" she asked. "Come closer so I can see you."

"It is I, Pip," I said, and entered the room.

"Thank you for coming," she replied.

I brought a chair to the hearth and sat down. Miss Havisham looked scared!

"I am not made of stone, you know," she began. "Can you believe that there is anything human in my heart?"

She stretched out her hand, but pulled it back before she touched me.

"If you can ever forgive me, pray do it!" she said. "Even if it is years from now and my broken heart is dust."

"Miss Havisham," I said. "I forgive you now. I need forgiveness, too, for the hurt I've caused others."

"If I could undo what I have done to Estella, I would," cried Miss Havisham. She wrung her hands in despair. "I regret it! I regret it so much!"

"Whose child is Estella?" I asked gently.

Miss Havisham shook her head.

"You don't know?"

She shook her head again.

"Mr. Jaggers brought her, didn't he?"

"Yes," she said. "Jaggers brought her to me when she was only two or three. I called her Estella. Her real mother had been charged with murder. Jaggers was her lawyer. He didn't tell me anything else about her mother—not even her name."

Miss Havisham and I parted at twilight. The dying light matched my mood. In the courtyard, I turned to take a last look at the old house.

Flames were shooting up in the window of the banquet room! I took the stairs two at a time and burst into the room.

Miss Havisham's faded wedding dress had caught fire! She was shrieking, "Fire! Fire! Save me!"

I threw my coat over her and pushed her to the floor, hitting at the flames. But it was not enough!

I swept the table clear of its feast. The rotten wedding cake smashed to the floor. I wrapped Miss Havisham in the tablecloth.

She screamed like a wild animal. She tried to break free, but I held her tightly.

At last the fire was out. Only smoke and cinders were left. Miss Havisham lay unconscious beside me.

For the first time, I became aware of my hands. They were burned raw from the fire. The pain was unbearable.

A doctor soon arrived and wrapped my hands. We put Miss Havisham to bed. She was weak with shock. And her burns were serious. Still, we hoped she would be fine with rest.

Before leaving, I whispered in her ear, "I forgive you." I hoped she heard me.

Chapter Eleven

Magwitch Is Free

My left arm was burned all the way to the shoulder. My right arm was not as bad. Herbert helped me change the bandages.

"Last night Magwitch told me that he had been married," he said as he wrapped a clean bandage around my arm. "His wife was jealous. They say she murdered a woman."

"How? When?" I asked, excited.

"Jaggers took the case," replied Herbert. "No one saw the crime. She didn't have to go to jail. She and Magwitch had a child who was about your age when he met you in the churchyard. You reminded him of his lost child. That is one of the reasons why Magwitch helped you all these years."

I felt feverish. My breath came in short gasps.

"Herbert," I said, "I think the man we are hiding is Estella's father!"

I went to see Jaggers the next day. I had to know the truth.

"Miss Havisham told me you brought her a child," I said. "She never knew who the mother was, but I do. I saw Estella's mother in these rooms just two days ago."

Mr. Jaggers said nothing. He was looking at the toes of his boots.

"Really?" he said finally.

I told him Magwitch's and Miss Havisham's stories.

"Pip," he said at last, "there are thousands of poor children living in the street. I thought if I could just save one life, it would be performing a miracle. This child was the one I decided to save.

"Her father was in and out of jail.

Her mother was accused of a crime. I cleared the woman's name and she gave me the child. I found the little girl a home. I gave the woman a job. The secret was mine alone. Now it is yours as well."

At last I knew the truth.

Monday morning I awoke with a fever. My left arm was swollen and very red. The pain was great. I could not stand to have anyone touch it.

I slept for two days. Herbert changed my bandages every few hours. He gave me cooling drinks. We both knew I had to be well enough to board the steamer out of England with Magwitch on Wednesday.

Our friend Startop had agreed to help row the boat out to the steamer.

On Wednesday, the sun shone hot, and the wind blew cold. It was March. I wore a heavy coat and carried one bag. My left arm was in a sling.

We rowed downstream to Mill Pond Bank. Magwitch was waiting for us. He quickly jumped into the boat.

"Dear boy!" he said, putting his arm on my shoulder. "Faithful dear boy, well done. Thankee! Thankee!"

Herbert and Startop rowed and rowed until the sun went down. We needed to be far down the river to catch the steamer.

"What freedom!" cried Magwitch. "How grand it is to sit next to my dear boy and have a smoke. The four walls were making me sick."

"If all goes well," I said, "you will be free and safe in just a few hours."

Soon night fell. The moon was full. We waited in the boat, shivering. It was half past one when we finally saw the smoke of the steamer.

Magwitch and I got our bags. I said a tearful good-bye to Herbert. We waited for the steamer to get closer. We would call for the captain to let us aboard.

Suddenly another boat shot out from the bank. It had been waiting in the shadows. There were three men on board. One of them was a policeman. He stood up and shouted, "You have an escaped convict in your boat! His name is Abel Magwitch. Arrest that man!"

The boat crashed right into ours. Compeyson stood on the deck of the other boat! And the steamer was still moving toward us!

Magwitch jumped at Compeyson, and the pair fell overboard into the river. They struggled for a moment, and then they both went underwater. We scanned the river for a sign of either man.

At last I spied a man swimming. It was Magwitch! The policeman grabbed him and hauled him into the boat. Chains were quickly locked to his wrists and ankles. He was captured!

Magwitch was badly hurt. A broken rib had injured one of his lungs, and he had a deep cut on his head.

Compeyson was dead. He had drowned.

I went with Magwitch to the prison in London. It was my place to stay by his side.

I did not fear or hate him anymore. He had been generous and loving to me through many years. He was better to me than I had been to Joe.

In prison, Magwitch grew very ill. I visited him every day. Though his face was pale, his eyes lit up whenever I entered his cell. He could only whisper his fears and regrets. He was always so tired.

The court found Magwitch guilty of murder. The police didn't believe that Compeyson had drowned accidentally. Magwitch would remain in jail for the rest of his life. He grew sicker, and I knew the end was near.

"Pip," he said as I sat down by his bed one morning. "Are you always the first visitor through the prison gate?"

"Yes," I said. "I don't want to lose a minute of time."

"Thankee, dear boy, thankee," he replied. "God bless you! You've never deserted me, dear boy."

I pressed his hand.

"Are you in much pain today?" I asked.

"Don't worry, dear boy," he said, and fell against the pillow. He was too weak to speak another word.

The guard made a noise outside the cell. My visiting time was over.

"Dear Magwitch, can you understand what I am saying?" I asked.

His pale eyes stared at the ceiling. He pressed my hand.

"You had a child once. You loved her but lost her," I said.

He pressed my hand even harder.

"She is living now. She is a beautiful lady. And I love her!" I blurted out.

Magwitch raised my hand to his lips.

He looked peacefully up at the ceiling. Then, quietly, his head dropped onto his chest. It was over.

I said a final good-bye to my dear Magwitch.

Chapter Twelve

A Healing Hand

With Magwitch gone and Herbert away on business, I was sick, lonely, and poor. My head felt like lead. My arms and legs ached. I lay on the sofa for days in a semi-delirious state.

One day two men came to collect money I owed for a bill. But I didn't have any money to give them. I didn't work. My only income had been Magwitch's money. The men asked me to come with them.

"I would if I could," I said. "But I might die on the way."

I did not hear their reply. My mind sank under the flood of my fever. For days I was without reason.

I dreamed about Joe. Once I opened

my eyes in the night and saw Joe seated in a chair by my bed. It was such a strange dream.

Once in the day, I opened my eyes and saw Joe sitting in the window seat. He was smoking his pipe and reading one of my books.

I asked the ghost if he would bring me a cold glass of water. The hand that gave me the drink was Joe's.

At last, I awoke and said, "Is it you, Joe?"

I heard his dear old voice answer, "Yes, old chap."

"Oh, Joe, you break my heart!" I replied. "I've treated you terribly. Don't be so good to me!"

Joe laid his hand on my forehead and looked into my eyes.

"We're old friends, dear Pip," he said. "I would do anything for you, anything at all."

"Have you been here the whole time, Joe?" I asked.

"Pretty much, old chap," replied Joe. "We got a letter telling us about your illness. Biddy told me to take as much time as was needed to get you well again."

"Is Miss Havisham dead, Joe?" I asked. I did not know if she recovered from the fire.

"She died a week after you took ill," Joe replied.

"What happened to her property and her riches?"

"Most of her money went to Estella," said Joe, as I slipped back into sleep.

Slowly my health returned. Joe took such good care of me that I felt as if I were a little child again.

One day he carried me outside to an open carriage. We drove out into the country to enjoy the sweet smells of summer.

Finally, I could take a few steps on my own.

"See, Joe!" I cried. "Soon I will walk again."

"Do not overdo it, Pip," said Joe. "But I shall be happy to see you up and about, sir."

Joe's last word upset me. It seemed that the better I got, the more strangely Joe treated me.

One night Joe asked me, "Are you stronger, old chap?"

"Yes, dear Joe, I'm getting stronger every day thanks to you."

The next morning Joe was gone. He had left a note that said I was well enough to live my life as a gentleman again, and he did not want to be a bother to me. He was going back home where he belonged. His note was signed "Ever the best of friends."

With the note was a receipt for my bills. Joe had paid them all!

What could I do but follow him to the forge? I wanted to thank him. And I planned to ask Biddy to marry me.

Maybe she would forgive me, if she saw that I had changed. We could make a good life together.

Three days later, I stepped onto the marshes again. I walked to the forge and listened for Joe's hammer. But the forge was dark. The door was locked.

The windows of the house were full of flowers. When I knocked, Biddy opened the door with a cry of surprise. Joe was beside her. They were both dressed in their Sunday best. And they both looked so very happy.

"It's my wedding day!" cried Biddy joyfully. "I am married to Joe!"

I was thankful that I had not told Joe of my plan to marry Biddy. They were both so excited to see me. I could not spoil their happiness.

"Dear Biddy," I said, "you have the best husband in the whole world. You should have seen how he took care of me.

"And, dear Joe, you have the best wife in the whole world. She will make you as happy as you deserve to be. You good, noble Joe!

"I am leaving England today. Thank you for all you have done for me! I owe you my life. I will not rest until I have paid back the money you spent to pay my bills.

"I hope you have a child. May the little fellow sit by the fire in winter and remind you of me.

"Don't tell him I was mean. Tell him that I loved you both because you were so good and true. I know your little fellow will grow up a much better man than I did."

I sold all my belongings and joined Herbert's company abroad. In two months, I was a clerk. In four months, I had my first raise.

The years went by, and I was made a partner. I was left in charge when Herbert went back to England to marry. He returned with his wife, Clara, and the three of us lived happily together.

It was eleven years before I saw Joe and Biddy again.

Chapter Thirteen

A Happy Ending

One December evening I put my hand on the latch of the old kitchen door and looked in.

Biddy sat by the fire, knitting, as she did years ago. Joe sat smoking his pipe at the kitchen table. His hair was a little gray but he was as strong and healthy as ever. Sitting on my own chair was a small boy who looked just as I had.

Joe was delighted to see me.

"The boy's name is Pip for your sake, dear old chap," said Joe. "We hope he grows up a bit like you."

I took young Pip for a walk the next day. We climbed the hill to the church-yard. I showed him my mother's and father's tombstones. I told him the story of what had happened to me so many years ago.

At dinner Biddy asked me why I'd never married.

"I am so settled in Herbert and Clara's home," I told her. "I am so used to my own ways."

"Dear Pip," said Biddy, for she knew my heart. "Do you think of her often?"

"That poor dream is over, Biddy," I said. But I knew I would visit Miss Havisham's house again for Estella's sake.

Estella's marriage had ended in separation. She had been so unhappy with Drummle! Two years ago he had been killed by a horse he was beating.

After dinner I walked to the old spot. The house and the other buildings were all gone. Only the crumbled rock of the old garden wall was left. I pushed open the rusted iron gate and went in.

I walked in the twilight. Memories of the old days drifted through my mind.

Suddenly I saw someone coming toward me down the garden path!

"Estella!" I cried.

"I am greatly changed," she said. "It's a wonder that you know me."

The freshness of her beauty was gone. But there was a new beauty. Her once-proud eyes were sadder, softer.

We sat down on a nearby bench.

"How strange to meet you on the very spot where we first met so many years ago," I said.

"Poor, poor old place!" said Estella. "The ground belongs to me, but little by little I had to sell everything else. Do you still live abroad?"

"Yes," I replied.

"And you do well, I am sure."

"I work hard and, yes, I do well."

"I often think of you," said Estella.

"Do you?" I replied.

"I think about what I threw away," she said. "I did not know true worth. Suffering was my teacher.

"My own heart has been bent and broken into a better shape, I hope. Tell me we are still friends."

"We *are* friends," I said, rising from the bench. "You have always had a place in my heart."

"We will continue to be friends then," said Estella, smiling.

The evening mists were rising. I took her hand in mine, and we went out of that ruined place. I knew we would never part again.

Charles Dickens was born in England in 1812. Dickens loved to write. When he was a teenager, he became a newspaper reporter. His experiences at the paper later helped him to develop realistic characters, conversations, and settings in his books. One of his early works, *The Pickwick Papers*, brought him worldwide fame when he was only twenty-four years old.

Dickens is one of the most highly regarded writers in English literature. He wrote twenty novels and many nonfiction books. Some of his best-known works are *A Christmas Carol*, *David Copperfield*, *Great Expectations*, *Oliver Twist*, and *A Tale of Two Cities*. Dickens died in 1870.

Monica Kulling was born in British Columbia, Canada. Ms. Kulling is the author of the Bullseye adaptations *Little Women*, *Les Misérables*, and *The Adventures of Tom Sawyer*. Her credits also include three picture books, many poems published in *Cricket* magazine, and several poetry anthologies. She lives in Toronto, Canada, with her partner and their two dogs, Sophie and Alice.

Collect the entire STEP INTO CLASSICS™ series!

You can find more Step into Classics™ wherever books are sold...

OR

*You can send in this coupon (with check or money order)
and have the books mailed directly to you!*

☐   THE ADVENTURES OF TOM SAWYER (0-679-88070-4) $3.99
☐   ANNE OF GREEN GABLES (0-679-85467-3) $3.99
☐   BLACK BEAUTY (0-679-80370-X) $3.99
☐   GREAT EXPECTATIONS (0-679-87466-6) $3.99
☐   THE HUNCHBACK OF NOTRE DAME (0-679-87429-1) $3.99
☐   KIDNAPPED (0-679-85091-0) $3.99
☐   KNIGHTS OF THE ROUND TABLE (0-394-87579-6) $3.99
☐   THE LAST OF THE MOHICANS (0-679-84706-5) $3.99
☐   LES MISÉRABLES (0-679-86668-X) $3.99
☐   A LITTLE PRINCESS (0-679-85090-2) $3.99
☐   LITTLE WOMEN (0-679-86175-0) $3.99
☐   MYSTERIES OF SHERLOCK HOLMES (0-394-85086-6) $3.99
☐   OLIVER TWIST (0-679-80391-2) $3.99
☐   PETER PAN (0-679-81044-7) $3.99
☐   PINOCCHIO (0-679-88071-2) $3.99
☐   ROBIN HOOD (0-679-81045-5) $3.99
☐   THE SECRET GARDEN (0-679-84751-0) $3.99
☐   THE THREE MUSKETEERS (0-679-86017-7) $3.99
☐   THE TIME MACHINE (0-679-80371-8) $3.99
☐   TREASURE ISLAND (0-679-80402-1) $3.99
☐   20,000 LEAGUES UNDER THE SEA (0-394-85333-4) $3.99

Subtotal	$ _____
Shipping and handling	$ 3.00
Sales tax (where applicable)	$ _____
Total amount enclosed	$ _____

Name _____

Address _____

City_____**State** _____**Zip** _____

Make your check or money order (no cash or C.O.D.s) payable to Random
House and mail to: Bullseye Mail Sales, 400 Hahn Road, Westminster, MD 21157.

Prices and numbers subject to change without notice. Valid in U.S. only.
All orders subject to availability. Please allow 4 to 6 weeks for delivery.

**Need your books even faster? Call toll-free 1-800-793-2665
to order by phone and use your major credit card.
Please mention interest code 049-20 to expedite your order.**